MICK FLAHERTY

ONLY IN BRITAIN

You Couldn't Make it Up!

FLAHERTY
WILL GET YOU
EVERYWHERE
PUBLISHING

First edition

This book was professionally typeset on Reedsy.
Find out more at reedsy.com

To everyone in Britain who just needs a laugh, no matter your background or situation. That's the beauty of books... they're for all of us. I also dedicate this to my son, Conor, who I love with all my heart, and to everyone who's crossed paths with me. You've all shaped this in some way.

Contents

Foreword

by Conor Flaherty

Right, so he's got me doing this again.

I did the foreword for his first book, *Don't Volunteer for Anything*, and now here we are, round two. Apparently, I'm Dad's official intro writer. Great.

Dad probably wants me to say he's absolutely hilarious, that you should definitely buy this book, and that he's the funniest person alive. Thing is, he genuinely believes that. He says it out loud in public, and with confidence.

Truth is, I'm funnier. He just hasn't come to terms with that yet. But I'll give him this; even in real life, when he's not banging on about whatever weird chapter he's writing that day, he is pretty funny. It kills me to admit it, but the bloke can write.

So yes, enjoy the book. Laugh at it, laugh with it, whatever. Just don't tell him I said anything nice. I'll deny it.

— *Conor*

Preface

So here we are again. Book number two.

The first one — *Don't Volunteer for Anything* — somehow became a number one bestseller on Amazon in satire, comedy, parody, and probably "books your uncle would read." It was mostly about military life, full of puns, pain, and at least one chapter involving a tactical tea break. For reasons I'll never understand, it flew.

But this one? This one's for everyone.

You don't need to have been shouted at by a Sergeant Major to get it. This is just everyday Britain. The stuff we all deal with and pretend we don't notice. The train seats that are never empty. The weather chats that go nowhere. The apologising to furniture. The eternal bin day guessing game. It's all here.

Each chapter is a snapshot of that specific kind of British nonsense we all put up with, never talk about properly, and definitely judge other people for. It's not political. It's not highbrow. It won't change your life. But it might make you laugh out loud while reading it in the bog or at your desk when you're meant to be working.

This book is basically a written shrug, but a very observant one. So whether you're northern, southern, skint, loaded, miserable, cheerful, or just wondering why we keep our tea bags in old biscuit tins, there'll be something in here you've said, done, or muttered under your breath in Tesco.

If you've bought this book online, please, for the love of Greggs and delayed parcel deliveries, leave a review. You don't need to write an essay. Just a quick "funny book, didn't hate it" will do the job.

Cheers,

Mick Flaherty, Amazon #1 Bestselling Author (no pressure)

I

ONLY IN BRITAIN

If you've ever said "sorry" to an inanimate object or stood in a queue without knowing what it's for, read on...

1

The Bag of Bags Under the Sink

Every home in Britain has one. It's not discussed. It's not proudly displayed. But it's there. A plastic bag full of other plastic bags, shoved under the sink next to some leaking bleach and a bottle of window cleaner that's mainly just water now.

You didn't set out to build this bag collection. It just happened. One day you bought milk, forgot your bag for life, and paid the 30p in shame. Then you did it again the next week. Before long you had enough to open a small market stall in 1993.

You always say you'll reuse them. That's the lie we all tell. You'll take them next time. Fold one up, shove it in your coat pocket, be prepared. But you don't. No one does. You go out, buy three things, say "nah I'll carry it" and end up juggling chicken thighs, onions and loo roll as if you're in a circus act outside Co-op.

Meanwhile, the Bag of Bags lives on. You don't throw it away, obviously. What if you need one? You never do, but the possibility keeps it alive. And it's not just one bag anymore, it's layers. There's the strong Tesco one you keep for potatoes. The thinner one that's got a hole in the corner but you use it for dirty washing. One that says "Morrisons" but you haven't been in Morrisons since the last Olympics. It's a collection. A time capsule of poor planning and supermarket shame.

When someone offers you a bag at the till, you still say yes. Not because you need it, but because saying no would mean fishing one out from the depths of your coat, unfolding it with a rustling shame and trying to act like the sort of person who's got their life together.

You don't. You've got 53 bags in a cupboard and still paid for another one today.

And you'll do it again next week. Because you're British. Because it's too much effort to sort them. Because you genuinely believe that one day, there'll be a moment when 40 flimsy plastic bags come in handy and you'll be glad you kept them.

You won't. But the Bag of Bags stays.

It's not hoarding. It's tradition.

2

Back in 5 (ish)': The Shopkeeper's Oath

You walk up to the door, try the handle, nothing. Closed. But not closed closed. Just temporarily gone. And there it is. The note.

"Back in 5 mins (ish)"

Brilliant.

It tells you everything and absolutely nothing at the same time. Could be two minutes. Could be Wednesday. You've now got a decision to make: do you wait? Do you loiter? Do you do that weird fake pacing thing people do when they're pretending they've got somewhere to be?

You peer through the window. It's empty. Light on, till open, a half-drunk bottle of Lucozade on the counter. No sign of life. You stand there looking like a lemon, trying to work out what '(ish)' means in this context. Is that 5 minutes real time, or 5 minutes British time, where everything takes just a bit longer than it should?

You look at your phone. Three minutes pass. Another bloke turns up.

"Is it shut?"

You both stare at the sign as if it's a cryptic crossword.

"Back in 5 (ish)."

He does the nod. You both pretend it makes sense.

Then comes the moral question: how long do you give it before you give up? Eight minutes? Twelve? It's not like anyone's coming out to update you. You're at the mercy of a scribbled ballpoint promise written on the back of a Cornflakes box.

Eventually, someone returns. No apology. No rush. Just a "Alright?" like they've been out for twelve seconds and not even a full episode of Tipping Point. You smile. You say nothing. Even though you've aged three years outside the door and are now rethinking your entire purchase.

That's the thing about the "5 (ish)" sign. It's not rude. It's just vague enough to be bulletproof. It's the perfect loophole. You can't be annoyed. It did say ish. And that's the most British thing of all — making lateness polite by slapping brackets around it.

3

Socks and Sandals: A British Cry for Help

There's a moment in every British summer where someone just gives up.

They open the wardrobe. They look at their battered trainers. They glance down at their feet and think, "No. Not today."

And they do it. They reach for the sandals. But they're not ready for barefoot. No one ever is.

So they add socks.

White ones. Ribbed. Possibly sports socks. Possibly thermal. Pulled all the way up, because apparently dignity is optional.

And out they go. To the shop. To the garden centre. To pick up a parcel from the post office. Walking around looking as if they've escaped a care home and no one's noticed.

And the worst part is: they're confident.

You point it out.

"You alright there, Dad?"

He shrugs. "They're comfy."

Right. Well, so are pyjamas but we're not all turning up to Asda dressed for bedtime.

It's always men over 50. Usually wearing cargo shorts with too many pockets and a T-shirt from a 10K they didn't actually run. One hand holding a pint, the other holding a barbecue tong, shouting "leave it, it's fine" while the chicken's still raw.

And look... this isn't a fashion statement. This isn't ironic. It's not edgy. It's pure utility. It's someone saying, "I want to feel the breeze, but not that much."

It's British stubbornness in outfit form.

Because deep down, we all want to be comfortable. We all want to free the toes. But we're scared. Of cold patios. Of gravel. Of showing too much skin and being judged by Janice next door.

So the socks stay. And the sandals go on. And we pretend nothing's wrong.

But we all know what's happened.

Someone's quit. They've surrendered to the weather. To the season. To life.

And do you know what?

Fair play.

Still looks awful, though.

4

Sunday Roast or Nothing: A Nation's Unspoken Rule

There are meals you plan, and then there's the Sunday roast, which just happens. You don't sit down and think, "What shall we have?" You wake up Sunday morning and somehow already know you're peeling spuds by 11.

You could be hungover, halfway through DIY, grieving, in love, mid-divorce, it doesn't matter. The roast happens. Beef, chicken, pork, nut loaf. Doesn't matter what. As long as there's gravy, roast potatoes, and something green that gets ignored.

The whole house smells of it by lunchtime. You open the oven door and get a steam facial. The meat's still frozen. You forgot carrots. There's only one Yorkshire pudding left in the freezer and it's fused to a bag of peas. Doesn't matter. We move forward.

The timing's always wrong. The potatoes are nearly done, the chicken's still pink, the gravy's boiling over, and someone's shouting, "Get the plates warm!" thinking it's an emergency.

You serve it up. It's fine. It's never hot.

One roastie's perfect. The rest are dark brown anxiety. Broccoli's been boiled into submission. Someone's moaning about the lack of stuffing. You tell them to stuff it.

Gravy saves it. Gravy covers all sins. You could serve shoe leather and a wet Jaffa Cake and if you drown it in Bisto, someone'll say, "Lovely, this."

Roasts aren't just about food, anyway. They're a national anchor. Something to sit round, moan about the week, talk about bin day, argue about whether cauliflower cheese counts, and bond over the shared trauma of running out of mint sauce.

And then, five minutes after eating enough to knock out a medium horse, someone says:

"What's for pudding?"

What's for pudding? You've just eaten your body weight in meat.

But fine. Sticky toffee it is.

Then you fall asleep on the sofa, trousers unbuttoned, watching Countryfile and questioning your existence.

And even if it was average. Even if the meat was dry and the sprouts were soap. You still say the same thing as you scrape the plates:

"Can't beat a roast."

We all know full well you can.

5

Apologising to Strangers and Inanimate Objects

I walked into a bin the other day. Said sorry to it. Not even quietly. Full volume. "Oh, sorry mate." It didn't reply, obviously, because it's a bin. But for that brief moment, I meant it.

This is life in Britain. We apologise to anything. Lamp posts. Bus stops. Fire doors. Once I said sorry to a coat stand because I thought it was a person. It had a hat on. Easy mistake.

It starts young. One minute you're a toddler throwing mashed potato at the wall, next thing you know you're six years old saying "sorry" to a table you've just bumped into. And your mum's nodding proudly as if you've just nailed diplomacy.

We don't just apologise for accidents. We apologise for *existing*. Trying to get past someone in the supermarket? "Sorry." Trying to leave a packed pub? "Sorry." Someone opens a door and smacks you in the face? Still "sorry." We apologise as if we're in a courtroom and the judge is always watching.

If someone walks straight into you on the high street, nine times out of ten, it's *you* who says "sorry." Why? Because we've got this national fear of being seen as impolite. We'd rather accept blame for someone else's mistake than risk being accused of confidence.

There's also the "Sorry Shuffle" – that weird half-step you do when you and another person try to pass each other and end up doing that awkward side-to-side dance like you're about to start a rumba. And what do you both do? You apologise. Then you both do it again. And again. Until someone blurts "sorry!" loud enough to break the spell and one of you scuttles off like you've just committed a minor crime.

It gets worse with technology. You ever bumped into someone while both of you are looking at your phones? That's double apology territory. One verbal, one with the awkward smile. That smile says, "I'm British and I've just inconvenienced another human being. Please forgive me. I'll go live in a bin now."

Even objects that *wrong* us get an apology. Stub your toe on the bed? "Sorry." Trip over the hoover you left in the hallway? "Sorry." You're apologising for not having the reflexes of a ninja, to furniture you bought yourself.

Then there's group apologies. Someone says they're cold and suddenly three people in the room apologise for the window being open, for not noticing sooner, and for existing near a draught.

We've turned "sorry" into a full-blown lifestyle. It's not

just a word here. It's a social lubricant. It replaces anger, confrontation, and conversation. It's how we start interactions and how we end them. It's how we let someone know we'd rather chew gravel than cause them even a whisper of inconvenience.

And yet, the best bit? If someone *doesn't* say sorry, we notice. "Bit rude," we think, from our place of moral high ground, having just apologised to a door.

Only in Britain can you get hit in the face by a rogue umbrella, drop your meal deal, step in a puddle, and still walk away mumbling "sorry" like *you* were the one out of order.

It's not madness. It's manners. And it's ours.

6

Saying "I Might Head Off" and Then Taking 40 Minutes to Actually Leave

There's a moment in every British gathering where someone stands up, claps their hands once and goes,

"Right... I might head off."

Now, that sentence does not mean "I am leaving."

It means "I have begun the delicate, slow-moving social ballet that may eventually lead to me being outside."

You're not going anywhere fast.

First, someone says, "oh already?" as if you've committed treason.

You now feel guilty despite having spent four hours here, two of them listening to Geoff talk about his back. You sit back down briefly while explaining, "yeah, just got a few bits tomorrow", which is code for absolutely nothing but you're emotionally done.

Then you do the coat shuffle. Not wearing it yet... just locating it. Possibly picking it up. Holding it in that classic 'I'm-about-to-go-but-not-yet' fashion, where it drapes over one arm while you keep talking about something pointless,.

Then there's the goodbye tour. You can't just wave and leave. You've got to speak to every single person who's still upright. You say goodbye to Lisa three times because she keeps restarting conversations and you're too polite to shut her down.

At some point you make it to the hallway. You put your shoes on while still talking.

This bit is crucial — you're now one foot in and one foot out, literally.

You lean on the bannister. You're still in full flow about how ridiculous it is that petrol's gone up again even though you've got no plans to go anywhere.

Then comes the door hover. Door's open. Coat's on.

Someone says something mildly interesting — "we should all go away for a weekend sometime" — and you're right back in it, mate.

You're now stood with your keys in one hand and a Lidl carrier bag in the other, discussing holiday cottages you'll never book.

Eventually, you make it to the pavement. You wave, say, "right then," and finally, finally start walking.

Only to turn back and shout "send me that thing you were on about" while pointing vaguely at no one in particular.

And that, my friend, is how you turn a simple goodbye into an endurance event that takes longer than the actual visit.

It's not leaving. It's an exit strategy, executed in phases. No one knows why we do it.

But if you ever say goodbye and leave within a minute, people will assume you're unwell or in trouble.

7

The National Suspicion of People Who Are Too Friendly Before 9 a.m.

There's something deeply untrustworthy about someone who greets you with too much energy before you've had a hot drink. It's not just odd, it's unsettling. You start questioning everything about them. Their motives, their background, whether they've done time. No one's that happy this early unless they're hiding something.

You could be stood at a bus stop, eyes barely open, mentally preparing for the day ahead, when some grinning maniac in a hi-vis gives you a hearty "Morning!" like it's an invitation to do star jumps.

You nod politely, obviously, because you were raised properly, but inside your brain's going, What the hell's he so cheerful about?

And it's not just at the bus stop. It's everywhere. Offices, shops, train platforms. Someone bounces in wearing a fleece and too much hope, saying "Alright, how are we today?" and you physically recoil. You're not ready for this level of social pressure. You've barely put your socks on properly. You've got toothpaste on your sleeve. You're still not sure what day it is.

The worst are the people who try to chat in a queue. Queue chat, before 9 a.m., should be a criminal offence. You're in Greggs. You've pointed at your bacon roll. You've done the bare minimum communication required to function. Then someone behind you pipes up with, "Lovely day, isn't it?" and you immediately suspect they work for the council or a cult.

And if someone says "Cheer up!" unprovoked, they're getting taken off your Christmas card list for life. You're not even miserable. You're just upright and breathing and trying to survive the morning without kicking off. That's a victory.

Look... most of us aren't miserable in the morning. We're just trying not to be visible. We're not ready for pleasantries. We don't want to talk about the weather yet. We don't want to be roped into a conversation about the gym routine of someone who's already had a smoothie and a 5K before you've even opened both eyes.

So yes, when someone's chirpy at 7:38 in the morning, we do look at them funny.

Not because they're happy.

But because we don't trust joy before daylight.

8

Weird Rules About Tea (Don't Get Them Wrong)

There's no official handbook on how to make tea in Britain, but every single one of us thinks our method is the correct one, and anyone who does it differently is either unwell or Australian.

The basics are simple, but even then, people have opinions. Mug, bag, boiling water, milk, maybe sugar. That's it. Or at least it should be. But you try doing that in someone else's house and watch how quickly the tension builds.

Boil the kettle — fine

Pour water on the bag — sure.

But when do you add the milk?

If you say "before the water," you're being watched. Your name's gone in a WhatsApp group. Milk first people aren't just wrong... they're dangerous. That's how it starts. First milk first, then pineapple on pizza, then they're storming Parliament.

Then there's brew time. Some leave the bag in for a precise 42 seconds. Others let it stew so long it could dissolve a spoon. You offer to make someone a cuppa and suddenly it's an interrogation.

"How do you like it?"

"Oh, not too strong. But not weak."

"Milk?"

"Just a splash."

"Sugar?"

"Half."

"Half?"

"Yeah, half a teaspoon. But not too much. Just enough to taste it but not taste it."

Right. Got it. So what you're asking for is... nothing specific, but very specific.

God help you if you're making tea at work. That's a political minefield. You ask if anyone wants one and suddenly you're writing down orders as if it's a takeaway.

Two milky, one builders, one with oat milk, one with two sweeteners but only if they're the pink ones, and one "just hot water" because someone's on a cleanse.

And then there's the moment of terror; you hand someone their tea, and they take that first sip. No words. Just a pause. A nod. Maybe a quiet "that's lovely". Or worse... silence. Just a sip and a smile that doesn't quite reach the eyes. That's your punishment for not reading their mind.

We don't do this with any other drink. You don't offer someone squash and have to guess whether they want "a smidge" or "like, proper strong." But with tea, we expect a stranger to know the exact shade of brown that means "perfect."

And no, herbal tea doesn't count. That's soup. Don't bring that near me.

Tea isn't just a drink here. It's currency. It's comfort. It's an apology, a celebration, a way to fill silence, and a coping mechanism when someone's just reversed into your fence. It fixes everything. Unless you make it wrong.

Then it ruins your entire day.

9

Greggs: A Cry for Help in a Paper Bag

Greggs isn't a bakery, it's a symptom. You're not popping in for a cheeky bite. You're dragging your half-dead body through the door because the day's already knackered and you need something you can eat with one hand while questioning your life choices.

It doesn't matter what time it is, Greggs will look exactly the same. No windows, no clocks, just a nuclear-lit beige bunker where pastry goes to die. You already know what's on the menu because it's the same as it was fifteen years ago. You don't browse. You point. You grunt. They hand it over wrapped in paper that's slowly turning translucent from mystery grease.

You eat it outside, in the rain, hunched on a bench that smells faintly of dog. You're surrounded by others doing the same; a community of defeated souls united by pastry and shame. There's a man in a tracksuit picking flakes out of his beard and a woman trying to feed a baby with one hand while eating a steak bake with the other. No one speaks. You're all in it together.

And yet, weirdly, no one complains. Because you know what? That sausage roll does the job. It might taste like cardboard and salt, but it fills the emotional hole. Greggs doesn't care about your nutritional needs or your self-worth. It just wants you back again tomorrow, broken and hungry, ready to queue behind three teenagers ordering seven doughnuts and a frozen latte at 8:47 in the morning.

10

Bin Day Confusion and Neighbourhood Surveillance

Bin day in Britain is less of a routine and more of a gamble. You might think you know the system. You might have a council calendar. You might even have an app. Doesn't matter. You'll still end up standing outside in your dressing gown, staring down the road at the neighbours' bins as though you're trying to crack a code.

Is it black this week? Is it recycling? Garden waste? Food caddy? That weird coloured one no one's touched since 2016?

So what do we do? We wait. Like absolute cowards.

You hover inside near the front window, pretending to tidy up but actually monitoring Carol from across the road to see what bin she puts out. Carol knows. Carol always knows. The minute she wheels out the green lid, there's a ripple of movement up and down the street. Similar to pigeons taking off at the same time.

"Green today, apparently."

Next thing you know, everyone's out dragging bins over gravel akin to the final event in some sort of passive-aggressive Olympic sport. But no one speaks. Just nods. Maybe a tight smile. All of us pretending we knew all along.

Heaven help you if you miss it. One day late and your bin's sitting there resembling a monument to failure while everyone else's are empty and back in place by 9am. You stand in the front garden, arms crossed, looking at it like it betrayed you personally.

The worst part? The council changes it all the time. Suddenly they're trialling a new scheme. Colour-coded food waste. Alternating fortnights. You get a leaflet through the door that explains it all in cheerful Comic Sans, but it might as well be written in Latin. You shove it in a drawer and forget it ever existed.

Then there's the bin men themselves. Olympic standard speed. They appear at 6:17am as though they're tactical unit, launching bags into trucks with the precision of a military drill. You hear them coming and leap out of bed in panic, dragging your bin down the drive as if you're a guilty criminal.

And don't act like you haven't done the bin panic sprint — barefoot, raincoat over pyjamas, trying to wheel it out just as the lorry turns the corner. The shame when they've already passed. That long walk back up the drive with a full bin and no dignity.

And yet, we never learn. We'll still be back at the window next week, peering through the blinds, waiting for Carol to make the first move.

Because Carol always knows.

11

Awkwardly Pretending You Didn't Just Let One Rip in Tesco

There's a moment. A brief, sharp moment. When you're in the household aisle, comparing fabric softeners, and it just... slips out. A small one. Unplanned. A real undercover agent.

You freeze. No one else is nearby. You think. You hope. You carry on.

Then you hear it. Trolley wheels.

A stranger approaches. They slow down. They're browsing. They pause.

You've got two options: walk away or hold your ground.

You panic. You pick up a bottle of bleach, pretending you were always going to spend 40 seconds reading the back of it.

The smell hits. It's not ideal.

You pull the classic British defence move: go completely still and do absolutely nothing. If you don't move, maybe they'll blame the smell on someone else. Maybe on themselves. Maybe on a product. There's always hope.

Then it happens. Eye contact. Just for a second. The silent standoff. They know.

You know they know. But we don't talk about it. Because this is Britain. And flatulence in a public setting is not a topic for discussion. We simply move on.

Maybe you add an extra item to your trolley to look busy. Maybe you leave the aisle altogether and go stare at toothbrushes you don't need. Maybe you whistle. But you do not acknowledge it. That would be worse than the crime itself.

The same rule applies in lifts, small shops, post office queues, and train carriages. If you accidentally let one go, your only real option is complete denial and, if necessary, framing a pensioner.

And if someone else lets one slip near you? You say nothing.

You leave them with their shame. Because next time, it might be you.

12

Moist: Britain's Most Hated Word

There are few words that cause national distress, but this one; this cursed, grim little syllable is responsible for more involuntary shudders than dentist drills and Ed Sheeran combined.

It's the sound. It's the texture. It's the way it clings to the roof of your mouth similar to week-old custard. You can say "damp" and get away with it. You can say "juicy," even though it makes you sound like a fruit advert. But drop "moist" into a conversation, and everyone in the room seizes up as if they've just witnessed a public accident.

It always shows up when you least want it. Cake adverts. Bad romcoms. Recipe books written by people who should frankly be on a list. You try to move past it, but it's there, squatting in your brain like an uninvited relative.

Bake Off's the worst. You're just trying to enjoy a bit of telly and suddenly someone's stood there saying, "This sponge is so moist" while Paul Hollywood stares at them as if they've just confessed to a murder.

We all hate it. No one says anything. But you feel the tension in the room. You feel your soul leave your body. It's ruined entire family meals. All because someone couldn't just say "not dry."

It's a linguistic grenade. And we all live in fear of when it'll go off next.

13

The British Way of Dealing with Compliments: Panic and Deflection

"That's a nice jacket."

Immediate internal meltdown.

Your mouth goes dry. Your hands forget what they were doing. You blurt out the first sentence that'll kill the compliment stone dead:

"Oh this? Got it in a sale. It was cheap. Nearly didn't bother."

Job done.

Because if there's one thing we can't handle, it's someone being genuinely nice to us. Compliments are treated like unsolicited mail — suspicious, uncomfortable, and best binned immediately.

We can't just say thank you. That would suggest confidence.

God forbid. Instead, we must explain the compliment away until it shrivels up and dies.

"Great haircut!"

"Oh, it's a bit short really. Think she went rogue with the clippers."

"You look smart!"

"Yeah well, had a funeral last week so thought I'd get the use out of it."

Even worse is when it's about something you made.

"These are lovely scones!"

"Oh they're overdone. Used the wrong flour. Should've chucked them really."

We do it automatically as though the compliment's a hot coal and we've got to bat it back as fast as possible. And it's not just deflection, it's competitive deflection.

Someone says,

"You're good at your job."

And we come back with...

"Not really. I just blag it mostly."

Then we both laugh and pretend it's all fine while silently wondering why we're like this.

We'd rather be roasted than praised. Someone insults your shoes? You'll banter back for hours. Someone says you look nice today? Full-body panic.

The only time we accept compliments is if it's about our tea-making skills.

"This is a good brew."

"Cheers."

Even then we'll mutter something about the teabags being on offer.

Compliments are like avocados: suspicious, slippery, and not part of our natural diet. Best handled with gloves and distrust.

14

"I'm Not Being Funny, But..." And Other Lies We Tell With Our Mouths

British people don't talk to communicate. We talk to avoid saying anything real. What comes out of our mouths has almost nothing to do with what we mean. It's all code. It's emotional Sudoku. Here's what we say, and what we actually mean:

"Not too bad, actually."

Translation: I've cried twice in a B&M car park this week and my boiler sounds haunted, but I'm still upright.

"Can't complain."

Translation: I absolutely can, I just can't be arsed going through the effort of being heard and ignored.

"It's not for me."

Translation: That was so awful it nearly ruined my weekend.

"Bit nippy, isn't it?"

Translation: I can no longer feel my kneecaps and may soon perish.

"I'll have to check my diary."

Translation: I'm not coming. I just need a polite gap between now and my eventual excuse.

"I don't want to be rude, but..."

Translation: Prepare yourself, I'm about to say something so rude it could get me barred from a funeral.

"Each to their own."

Translation: You're a wrong'un and I want no part in it.

"Well, that's different."

Translation: That's dreadful. I'm going to tell everyone what you've done.

"I might pop in later."

Translation: I'm absolutely not popping in. I've already taken my bra off.

"With respect..."

Translation: You're thick and your opinion should come with a warning label.

"Bless them."

Translation: They're clearly struggling but I'm not invested enough to intervene.

"It's a bit of a faff."

Translation: It involves more than one step, so I'm out.

"I'm sure it'll be fine."

Translation: We're all doomed but I'm trying not to cry in public.

"Fancy a brew?"

Translation: Let's stop whatever this is and re-centre our souls.

"Not my cup of tea."

Translation: I'd rather eat lint than pretend to enjoy this again.

"You alright?"

Translation: I'm not interested in your emotional state, this is just how I say hello.

"Could be worse."

Translation: I have completely given up but I still own a kettle, so life must go on.

We've built an entire culture around avoiding directness. If you say what you mean, people think you've got no filter. We don't hug. We nod. We text people we live with. And we use phrases that sound comforting but come with built-in insults, because if there's one thing we've mastered in this country, it's saying everything except what we're actually thinking, then sighing loudly until someone notices.

And if they ask if we're okay?

"Yeah, I'm fine."

Translation: I am definitely not fine. But thanks for asking.

15

"Go On, You Have It" – The Last Biscuit Stand-Off

There is no power struggle in Britain greater than the silent war over the last biscuit. You could leave a custard cream on a plate in an office kitchen for three weeks and nobody would touch it. Not because they don't want it, but because claiming it would officially make you selfish.

Nobody wants to be The One Who Took The Last Biscuit. That's how reputations die. That's how you end up uninvited to Denise's retirement do.

So we go into full social chess mode.

"Help yourself," someone says, leaning back, eyes flicking to the plate.

"Oh no, I'm alright," comes the reply, stomach growling, tears behind the eyes.

"You sure? Go on, have it."

"No, no. You have it. Honestly."

Then everyone just sits in tortured silence, watching the biscuit slowly go stale until Carol, the cleaner, eventually bins it with a muttered "bloody savages."

And it's not just biscuits. This nonsense extends to:

The last roast potato

Sat on its own, golden, crispy, calling out to you, but you've made the fatal mistake of going last. Now you've got to do the polite pause. "Anyone else want this?" you ask, hoping nobody answers, only for your mum to swoop in with "oh your Uncle Terry's only had three." So now it's Terry's potato. You get boiled carrots and the burden of being too well-mannered.

The last chip

You both saw it. You both know it's there. But someone's got to make the move. The real British solution? Suggest splitting it. One chip. Cut into two. Because nothing screams dignified nation more than halving a single McCain.

The last square of chocolate

The bar's been broken down into tiny economic segments. Each person's had a fair share. One square remains. If you eat it, you're greedy. If you leave it, you're a hero. So it stays there, uneaten, until it melts into the wrapper and someone blames the dog.

The final slice of cake

This is now sacred. No one can touch it. It is no longer food, it is ceremony. People will pass it round the table like it's a newborn, each person saying "no, I couldn't possibly," while mentally calculating the calories they've already inhaled.

It's a strange logic we've developed. We'll eat five biscuits in a row without blinking, but that sixth? That's the line. That sixth biscuit is morally wrong. It's betrayal, gluttony, and social suicide, all rolled into one crumbly custard-coated trap.

Nobody actually wants to be the martyr. We just want someone else to be the greedy one so we can all feel better about ourselves. So we leave it. We leave the final thing. The last crisp, the final Haribo, the smallest sausage roll. And then we moan we're still hungry and stare at it until someone gives in.

And when they finally do?

"Oh, I was going to have that."

You weren't. But now they feel awful and so the British cycle of guilt begins again. Tea solves it, usually. Until the biscuit plate comes out again. Then it starts all over.

God save the King. And the last Jammie Dodger.

16

Calling the Dog by Its Full Name When It's in Trouble

There's a very specific moment in every British household when the dog stops being "Bobby" and becomes "Robert Charles Barkington the Third, what do you think you're doing?"

It's always when something's been chewed, pissed on, or traumatised. That's when the dog hears its full title. You don't even remember giving it one, but somehow in that moment, you summon a name that sounds straight out of a 1920s school register.

"Archibald Rupert Flaherty, put that chicken down."

There's a tone shift too. Not shouting, not quite. It's that middle-class fury our parents perfected. The kind that could shame you into handing back a stolen Mars bar using nothing more than a full name and a raised eyebrow.

The dog doesn't listen, of course. It just stares at you with its tail wagging and half a sock hanging out its gob. You try again, this time slower, spacing out the syllables as if you're announcing the next contestant on *The Apprentice*. You're not even sure why. It's a Labrador. It barely knows its own name on a good day.

The full-name treatment is usually followed by a lecture. You speak to the dog like it's a small, idiotic flatmate who's just broken the telly and now refuses to make eye contact. You start pacing. You do that British thing where you talk to no one while tidying angrily.

"Unbelievable. Brand new. Straight out the bloody packet."

And yet, when they curl up later, still smelling of damp and bad choices, you forgive them. You look down and say "you little sod" with affection and scratch their ears like you haven't just spent the morning bleaching half the kitchen.

The dog, of course, has no clue what just happened. But it knows this much: if you're using its full name, it's either done something wrong or it's going to the vet.

Possibly both.

17

Using 'Each to Their Own' as a Polite Way of Saying Someone's an Idiot

Someone tells you they enjoy cold beans straight from the tin. Or that they don't drink tea. Or that they listen to podcasts at double speed while doing yoga and eating pickled eggs.

You look at them. You nod. You say the words.

"Each to their own."

What you mean is: That's the most ridiculous thing I've ever heard and I'll never respect you in the same way again.

But you say it kindly. Because that's what we do.

It's the British version of calling someone a lunatic without upsetting them. A verbal shrug that lets you back away from madness without starting a scene.

We deploy it in all sorts of situations:

45

– When someone says they love a six-hour coach trip

– When a mate's just paid £10 for milk and hot foam in a jam jar

– When your cousin brings homemade hummus to a barbecue.

– When someone openly admits they like Love Island "for the chat"

You hear it, you smile, you say it:

"Each to their own."

And move on with your life.

It's also handy when trapped in a conversation you want to escape. A bloke in the pub's explaining crypto, you've stopped listening, he's well into his third chart, and you just want out. You wait for a gap and hit him with:

"Ah right, yeah. Each to their own."

End of chat. You've escaped with dignity intact.

The genius of it is that it sounds accepting. It sounds tolerant. It gives the illusion of open-mindedness while being, in practice, the diplomatic equivalent of putting your phone down mid-conversation.

Because we'd never say,

"That's weird."

or

"You've lost the plot."

Not out loud, anyway.

We say,

"Each to their own."

Which really means:

"You crack on, but not near me."

18

Getting Home and Immediately Putting Pyjamas On, Regardless of the Time

You walk through the door. Keys down. Shoes off. The jeans? Gone. The bra? If applicable, flung. And within 90 seconds of arriving home, you are in pyjamas.

It doesn't matter what time it is. 5pm? Fine. 3pm? Also fine. Lunchtime? No one's judging.

Because once you're in the house, the rules of society no longer apply. You are free.

And freedom looks like a pair of bobbly Primark bottoms and a hoodie you wouldn't wear outside unless your bin was on fire.

You might still have things to do: emails, dinner, ironing, explaining to the cat why it's not allowed lasagna; but none of that's stopping the pyjamas.

We're not even talking about fancy pyjamas. These aren't the posh, matching kind. These are old. These are worn. These have memories. Possibly gravy stains. Possibly elastic that's long since given up.

Sometimes you don't even put the heating on. You just whack on the pyjamas and two pairs of socks and march around like a 19th-century coal man on their day off.

And it's not just about comfort. It's about mentally clocking out.

Outdoors = stress, people, trousers.

Indoors = elastic waistbands, horizontal lounging, snacks you didn't plan to eat.

It's especially British because we don't make a big thing of it. We don't say,

"I'm getting into my loungewear."

We just do it. We walk upstairs in jeans, and come back down in an outfit that screams I will not be answering the door after this.

And if anyone dares visit unexpectedly, they get what they get. You answer in your owl slippers and a dressing gown that's one wash from disintegrating. If they raise an eyebrow, you just say:

"Didn't know you were coming, did I?"

If you're in...

You're in pyjamas.

19

Someone's Sitting in the Seat You Did Reserve

There it is. Carriage B, Seat 34A. Reserved. Yours. It says so on your ticket. You triple-checked it. You're already picturing the smug sit-down. But as you turn the corner... someone's already in it.

Bag on the seat, coat half off, sandwich out, legs splayed. They've moved in.

You freeze. Everything in you says, "Challenge this." But the British side of your brain is already making excuses:

Maybe they didn't see the reservation.

Maybe they're only on for one stop.

Maybe confrontation is worse than standing for three hours near the loo.

You edge forward.

"Hi... sorry, I think that might be my seat?"

You even put a question mark on the end, as if there's room for debate.

They glance at you. Then your ticket. Then the screen above the seat that very clearly says "Reserved."

Then they say it. The sentence that's launched a thousand clenched fists:

"Is it alright if I just stay here?"

No. No it's not alright. But what do you say? You panic. You smile. You say:

"Yeah, no worries."

Then spend the rest of the journey standing by the bin, swaying with the train like an abandoned ghost.

If you do find the courage to say, "I'd rather sit in the seat I booked," they act shocked. As if you're the one being unreasonable. Like choosing the one place on this moving tin can where your legs won't cramp is some wild power trip.

Eventually they move. Slowly. With the air of a martyr. Muttering things under their breath. You sit down feeling like you've just committed a minor crime.

You spend the next 45 minutes apologising in your head for having the sheer audacity to sit where you were supposed to.

You don't feel victorious. You feel British.

20

British BBQs: Rain, Raw Chicken, and Regret

Every year, the sun peeks out for more than 40 minutes and the country collectively loses its mind.

Shorts are on. Paddling pools are dragged out of sheds. And somewhere, someone says the six words that have cursed a thousand weekends:

"We should do a BBQ, yeah?"

Should we? Really?

No one in this country is built for BBQs. It starts with hope. Someone nips to Asda and buys 48 sausages, a disposable tray of potato salad and a suspicious bag of charcoal that says "easy light" but hasn't lit easily since 1994.

Then the ritual begins. One man, *always* a man, takes up position at the BBQ with the tongs. He's never cooked a thing indoors but suddenly becomes Gordon Ramsay with smoke in his eyes. His job is to stand there, turning undercooked meat, poking flames, and saying things like *"should be alright in a minute"* even though it clearly isn't.

Half the guests hover around awkwardly, holding paper plates that can't support the weight of a single sausage. Someone tries to balance coleslaw on a lettuce leaf. Someone else opens a beer with their teeth. The dog's already nicked two burgers and thrown up near the patio door.

Then comes the weather. Always. What started as "glorious sunshine" has turned into *that* specific British drizzle; not full-on rain, just that thin, misty stuff that gets into your bones. But does anyone admit defeat? Of course not. We carry on, huddled under a flimsy gazebo from B&M, chewing lukewarm drumsticks while pretending this is fun.

The salads go warm. The bread rolls go damp. The crisps go soft. And the one veggie guest is sat there with a half-grilled mushroom and a haunted look in their eyes.

Someone's Nan turns up with a fold-up chair and a trifle, which immediately melts. A bee invades the hummus. The kids are crying because the Bluetooth speaker's run out. Someone shouts *"Did anyone bring ketchup?"* as if this wasn't the entire point of going to the shop.

And then, just as everyone's food-poisoned and the rain really sets in, someone always — *always* — says:

"We'll have to do another one soon."

Will we? Will we though?

21

Saying "We Must Catch Up Soon" With Absolutely No Intention of Doing So

You see them near the meal deals. An old mate from school. Or work. Or that one summer you did a 10k run. You lock eyes. Too late to escape.

There's a pause. The classic British reunion greeting:

"Blimey! Long time!" Followed by:

"How's things?" and

"You look well!"

No one ever says, "You look tired and slightly greyer." Even though they do.

You both do the polite catch-up routine. Work. Kids. Life. You nod a lot. Throw in a laugh that says "God, how time flies," even though you've spent the last five years actively avoiding situations just like this.

Then comes the closing line. The social parachute:

"We must catch up soon!"

You both say it at exactly the same time. With exactly the same lack of conviction.

No date is set. No actual plan is formed. There's no follow-up. There never will be.

You both know it's a lie. A kind, mutual, beautifully British lie that says, "This interaction is now complete, let's never do this again."

And the dance continues:

"Yeah, definitely."

"Let's sort something."

"We'll have to get a pint!"

Then you both back away like polite cowards. You pretend to look at salad. They pretend they forgot something in frozen veg. No one looks back.

It's not rude. It's not unkind. It's standard. Saying "we must catch up" is similar to saying "we'll put the heating on soon" — everyone knows it's not happening, and we're all fine with that.

It's the thought that counts. And the thought is:

"Let's keep this relationship exactly where it is; buried in shared history and vague fondness, never to be spoken of again."

Perfect.

22

The Art of the Passive-Aggressive Note

There's something deeply British about reaching breaking point and choosing to deal with it... by scribbling a note and sticking it somewhere visible with a bit of dignity and a lot of Sellotape.

We don't confront. We don't knock on doors. We don't raise voices. We get a passive-aggressive notepad from the back drawer, grab a pen that barely works, and let the frustration flow through handwriting that somehow gets angrier with every line.

"PLEASE do not take up TWO parking spaces."

"Bin collection is THURSDAY. Like it's always been."

"Your cat is using my garden as a toilet. This is not acceptable."

That last one was typed and laminated. Laminated. That's not just petty, that's commitment.

We never sign them either. Just a mysterious note, stuck under a windscreen wiper or blu-tacked to the communal fridge. No one admits to writing it, but everyone knows who it was. It's Sandra from number 3. It's *always* Sandra.

In shared houses, the fridge note is a classic. You eat someone's yoghurt and suddenly there's a passive-aggressive essay stuck next to the milk:

"To whoever ate my Müller Corner: I hope it was worth it. Some of us PAY for our food."

It's got bullet points, capital letters and a passive-aggressive smiley face at the end. **":)"**

Nothing says "we're at war" like a smiley that means "I'll never trust you again, Lisa."

The British note isn't about solving problems. It's about *broadcasting displeasure* in the most indirect way possible. You're not talking to the person. You're addressing "whoever," "someone," or "this household." It's confrontation at arm's length, with a tone that says, *"I've had enough but I'm still polite enough to write this on lined paper."*

We also love underlining. And quotation marks that shouldn't be there.

"Please put your 'rubbish' in the bin."

What does that even mean? Why are we questioning whether

it's rubbish? It's clearly a crisp packet.

And there's always that one final line, the emotional kicker, designed to ruin your whole day.

"Some of us work full time."

"You wouldn't behave like this in your own home."

"Disappointed doesn't even cover it."

You don't sleep right for a week after reading that one. But the truth is, deep down, we *love* writing them. It's therapy. We won't say a word out loud, but we'll happily spend fifteen minutes constructing a note that makes someone else feel a carefully measured amount of guilt.

And when we're on the receiving end? We do exactly what's expected. We read it. We scoff. We fold it up. Then we immediately do whatever it told us not to, just with slightly more stealth.

It's the British way. We don't confront. We write politely aggressive notes and then go back inside to make tea and re-watch Deal or No Deal.

23

The Queue: Sacred, Silent, and Unquestioned

We don't have a national anthem that unites us. We have the queue.

Nothing defines Britain more. We'll queue for buses. For loos. For warm cans of lager at a festival. We'll queue for other queues. And we do it in total silence, bonded by an unspoken contract of mutual tolerance and mild resentment.

There's no sign, no instruction. We just know. You walk up, you find the end, and you join it. You don't ask questions. You don't push in. You accept your place in the grand order of things, even if it means waiting behind a bloke who's paying for chewing gum with coppers and sighing between each coin.

The queue is built on trust. Break that trust, and society unravels. Every Brit knows the feeling when someone walks up and sort of hovers near the front, pretending they haven't seen the line of 17 people already staring at them. No one says a word, of course. That would be *confrontation*. Instead, we all give them the full force of British fury: the long stare, the head tilt, the polite cough. Occasionally a theatrical sigh.

If things really kick off, someone might say, quietly but pointedly, *"Think there's a queue, mate."* That's DEFCON 1. If that doesn't work, we write about them in group chats for weeks.

We don't queue efficiently either. We queue emotionally. You'll see someone with one item stand behind a family with three trollies full of tins because it's the proper thing to do. Then we nod and say things like *"I'm not in any rush"* while internally preparing a full legal case for why the person in front should be deported for using self-checkout to do their monthly shop.

There's also Queue Maths. That moment when you try to assess which queue will move quicker. You pick the wrong one, obviously, but you stick with it because switching queues makes you a traitor. You'd rather waste 12 minutes out of sheer principle.

Sometimes you end up in a queue without even knowing what it's for. You just saw a line and thought, *"Well, must be worth it."* You could be queuing for soup or a tax audit. Doesn't matter. You've committed now.

It's a national skill. Other countries push. Other countries shout. We form a line and pretend we're fine, even if our legs are numb and the person in front is taking a phone call on speaker.

And when you finally get to the front, after all that waiting, do we celebrate? No. We say thank you. We take our receipt. And we leave the same way we came in.

Quiet. Polite. And absolutely fuming.

24

The 30p Bag Crisis: A National Reckoning

You reach the till. Arms full. Bread, toothpaste, four ready meals you're pretending are for the freezer, and a bottle of shower gel.

Cashier barely looks up.

"Need a bag?"

You pause. Everything inside you screams yes. But your mouth says,

"Nah I'm alright."

Because the shame of paying 30 pence for a bag now outweighs the practicality of having functioning hands.

So you do what we all do. Try to carry 14 items in two arms, no plan, no balance, just raw panic. One item under the chin. One pinched between elbow and ribs. A four-pint of milk tucked into your coat.

As you leave, wobbling through the sliding doors with your receipt in your mouth, you catch someone's eye and you know. You both know.

You should've just bought the bloody bag.

But no. Because 30p. Thirty Pence! For something that used to be free and now feels like you're taking out a loan.

And if you do cave and get one? It's never the normal kind. It's some rigid, glossy monstrosity that could hold patio slabs. Covered in beetroot-themed slogans and handles that feel like seatbelts from a Soviet bus.

You fold it neatly. Say "I'll reuse this one."

You won't.

You'll shove it under the sink with the 46 others. A cupboard full of ambition and lies.

Then next week, you'll be back in the shop, arms full, being asked the same question by a teenager who's already judged you.

And the cycle continues.

Because it's not just a bag. It's a test. And we keep failing it. Publicly. With biscuits under our armpit.

25

Coffee: You Don't Even Like It, Do You

You walk into the café and immediately regret it. Sorry, no. You walk into the café and immediately wish you'd stayed home with a tea bag and a bit of dignity. You're met with a menu written in curly chalk letters that look fancy but spell out pure nonsense.

You try to act natural. Everyone else seems to know what they're doing. They're ordering flat things, long things, cold things with cream on top and plant milk. You step up and say "just a coffee." The barista pauses. Asks you what kind. You say "a normal one," which somehow makes things worse.

You end up with something you didn't ask for in a cup you can't hold. Your name's been written wrong on it, probably as "Nuck" or "Mig," and now you're stood in a corner holding a paper cup that cost five quid and tastes like soil and confusion.

Around you, everyone's playing along. A woman's pretending to enjoy a drink that looks like sun cream. A bloke's staring at his laptop, no idea what he's doing. There's a toddler in a pram holding a babycino with more confidence than you've had all week.

You spot the sugar tray. Tiny wooden stirrers, oat milk, six sachets of brown powder pretending to be cane sugar, and one lonely packet of actual sugar someone's already half-used and folded back in.

You sit down. The seat's a wooden cube. Your knees touch. There's music playing, sounding like a banjo falling down some stairs. You try to drink what you've bought. It's too hot. You try again. It's cold. There was no in-between.

And still, you smile. You nod. You walk out with the cup in your hand as if it's a prop. You might as well be carrying a traffic cone for how useful it is. But you do it. Because everyone else is doing it. And deep down, you think, maybe next time it'll taste alright.

It won't.

26

Weather Chat: The Official Language of Britain

There are only three guaranteed things in this country: the DFS sale always being on, someone having opinions about crisps, and weather chat.

You can spot two Brits meeting for the first time by how quickly someone says, *"Bit muggy today."* That's not small talk. That's a handshake, a signed contract, and a blood oath all in one. Once the weather's been acknowledged, we're allowed to proceed with the rest of the interaction. And it's not just a passing comment. It's an entire national script.

"Bit cold out, isn't it?"

"Aye, it's that damp cold though. Gets in your bones."

"Still, better than yesterday."

"Oh yeah, that was miserable."

"They said it'd brighten up."

"Lied, didn't they."

"Always do."

We can go back and forth like that for twenty minutes without repeating a line. There are regional variants too. Up north, it's more *"Fresh out there today."* Down south, it's *"Absolutely Baltic."* No one quite knows what that means, but we say it with authority.

We've all had a moment where we've walked outside, looked at the sky and said *"Ooh, looks like rain,"* even when it's already raining. It's not information. It's instinct. Half the time we're already holding an umbrella while saying it.

Weather apps mean nothing here. You check it, it says sun, and five minutes later it's hailstones and the dog's blown over. So instead, we trust old-fashioned methods, e.g., how the wind smells, or what Karen from down the road said it "felt like" on her patio this morning.

It's also how we fill awkward silences. First dates, barber chairs, GP waiting rooms — just fire off a quick "can't make its mind up today" and watch the tension melt away. It's social glue.

The most British thing of all is when the weather *is* finally nice, and we still complain. Too hot. Too bright. Too sweaty. Tarmac's melting. People walking round as if they've never seen sunlight. "Bit much, this."

Then when it's gone, we mourn it in the style of a national tragedy.

"That was our summer, that."

"Blink and you miss it."

"Ah well. Back to normal."

And that's what it always comes back to. *Normal.* Mild. Damp. Cloudy.

Weather so unremarkable, we talk about it constantly.

And we wouldn't have it any other way.

27

Online Dating: Where British People Go to Lie Politely

Online dating, in this country, is just formalised small talk with pictures. It's a polite queue of people pretending they're easy-going, well-travelled, and don't own novelty socks.

You start by making a profile that isn't really you. It's the version of you who jogs twice a week, reads "a lot of thrillers," and enjoys meaningful chats on pub benches. None of which has ever happened.

Then you pick your photos. First one, decent lighting, preferably not holding a pint, though you are. Second one, you smiling next to a stranger's dog you said was yours. Then you throw in something 'fun', which is usually a photo of you near a waterfall looking slightly uncomfortable. You caption it with something hilarious you stole from Twitter in 2014.

Then the algorithm chucks you at the mercy of the local area. You're shown a mix of gym selfies, fish-holding men, women in festival hats, people standing on cliffs with captions that suggest they're "looking for someone to share the view."

You match with someone. You spend twenty minutes rewriting "Hey" to make it sound spontaneous. You settle on "How's your weekend going?" and instantly regret it. They reply six hours later with "Not bad, just cleaning the flat x.

What now? You're not built for this. You're built for awkward eye contact in supermarkets and realising someone fancies you because they once offered you a Polo.

Eventually you go on a date. It's at a pub you've never been to, where the chairs wobble and the menu includes artisan coleslaw. You sit across from someone who looks vaguely like their photo and discuss how much you "love travelling," despite the fact your passport's been expired since the referendum.

You both pretend this is going well. You both say, "We should do this again," which in Britain means "I will now quietly disappear into the internet, never to be seen again."

You go home. You delete the app. You redownload it two days later. You upload a new photo of yourself with a roast dinner and write "Not looking for anything serious...."

And round we go again.

28

Avoiding Eye Contact Since 1066

If two British people make eye contact on public transport, one of them has to move house.

We're not wired for it. Doesn't matter if you've known the person 20 years or you're sitting three feet away; once your eyes meet, it's full-body panic. You both immediately look away as if you've just witnessed something illegal. Then you spend the next three stops pretending to read the same sentence in *Metro*.

It's not that we're rude. It's that we live in constant fear of social obligation. Eye contact means you might have to nod. Or worse, smile. And that opens the door to a conversation, which leads to words, and before you know it, you've told a stranger your entire family history before 9am.

So we don't risk it.

The train is the main battleground. If you're sat opposite

someone, you lock in on a spot just to the left of their ear. You don't move. You don't blink. You'd rather stare out a pitch-black window and look at your own reflection than accidentally glance up and see another human.

Lifts are just as bad. Four people in a box, no one speaking, all staring at different corners as if they've just been caught shoplifting. Someone coughs and we all consider taking the stairs forever.

Even walking down the street, you do the head-tilt shuffle. You see someone from work coming your way. Too far away to ignore. Too close to fully blank. You make a quick decision to look at your phone, even though it's off, just to avoid the social choreography of a "hello."

Shops are worse. You see someone you vaguely know in the bread aisle and immediately duck behind the Warburtons as if you've gone into witness protection. You then spend the next ten minutes doing tactical loops around frozen veg, hoping they leave first. And when they do, you exhale like you've dodged a speeding fine.

It's not personal. We're just trying to get through the day without making it weirder than it needs to be.

And the best bit? If someone *does* make confident eye contact, we immediately think,

"Alright, what's *your* problem?"

Too much confidence. Suspicious. Probably from abroad.

It's not that we don't like people. It's just... we prefer them at a safe distance, slightly blurred, and preferably facing the other way.

That's the British way.

29

Bank Holiday Madness: DIY, Traffic, and Disappointment

There's a specific type of optimism in Britain that only shows up when the words Bank Holiday Weekend are mentioned. You could be dead behind the eyes the rest of the year, but as soon as someone says, "Three-day weekend coming up," your brain starts planning, akin to just been given freedom.

You imagine peace. Lie-ins. Sunshine. You tell yourself you'll finally get the garden sorted. Maybe even have people round. Bit of food. Nice drink. Sorted.

You absolute fool.

What actually happens is you wake up Saturday to drizzle, a wasp in the bedroom, and a suspicious smell coming from under the sink. You then spend 45 minutes in B&Q queuing behind a man who's buying 12 metres of skirting board and arguing with his wife about hinges.

If there's one thing we *all* do on a Bank Holiday, it's attempt DIY we're not qualified to do. Fence painting, shelf putting-up, flat-pack furniture that requires 16 screws and your soul. We tell ourselves, *"How hard can it be?"* as we hold a cordless drill as if we've never seen one before.

Then the rain starts. Obviously. Never just rain though; misty stuff that somehow soaks you even if you're under cover. You stand there with a roller in one hand, fence paint in your hair, staring at the sky, thinking it's personally let you down.

So you abandon the DIY and decide to *go somewhere* instead. Day trip. Change of scenery. You and 400,000 other idiots with the same idea. Every A road is blocked, every pub is full, every coastal town is packed with confused pensioners looking for public toilets.

You sit in traffic for an hour. One kid's crying, the other one's gone quiet in a worrying way, and the only food in the car is a half-melted chocolate bar stuck to a receipt.

Eventually you get there — beach, stately home, service station with aspirations — and it's worse than you imagined. £7 to park on a gravel pit. £4.50 for a sausage roll. You end up wandering round a gift shop full of tea towels you don't need, buying a jar of chutney out of guilt.

Then you drive home in silence, get in, and decide to *make the most of it* by cleaning the barbecue in the rain while muttering about how "we'll do something proper next time."

And on Monday night, as you sit there sunburnt, skint, and slightly injured, someone always says,

"Nice to have a break, though."

Is it?

30

No, After You: The Etiquette of Pointless Politeness

I went to the Co-op last week. Reached the door at the same time as a man carrying a crate of Diet Coke and the expression of someone halfway through a full mental collapse. We both stopped. Both smiled. He said, "After you."

I said, *"No, no, you go."*

He said, *"You sure?"*

I said, *"Yeah yeah, honestly."*

He said, *"Cheers."*

I said, *"No worries."*

Then we stood there. Both of us. No one moved. I could feel my own life ticking away. Eleven full seconds of eye contact, head tilts, and mutual panic until he cracked and speed-walked through as if he'd just stolen something. I followed immediately after and apologised.

This is what we do. We don't just go through a door. We perform a full social ceremony that involves deferring all basic movement until someone reacts first.

We say "after you" as if it's the law. Doesn't matter if you're in a car park, a narrow alley, a lift, or just both heading toward the same space at the same time. Someone has to say it. And once it's said, the other person is legally obligated to resist. You *must* both argue, just for a moment, about who should go. That's the ritual. It's not optional.

Sometimes it escalates. Two people both refusing to go first.

"Honestly, go."

"No no, you go."

"No I insist."

"Seriously, mate."

"Honestly, don't be daft."

You can lose entire afternoons like this. And then there's the group version. Four or five people all arriving at the same bottleneck. It becomes a polite Mexican standoff. Everyone waves everyone else forward. No one moves. One person tries to shuffle forward, but immediately gets guilt-shamed into stepping back again. At some point someone panics, says "Oh I'll just wait here," and pretends to check their phone until the coast is clear.

It's not about politeness. Not really. It's about avoiding the *appearance* of being forward. You could be desperate for a wee, bleeding slightly, and two steps from passing out; but if someone gestures for you to go first, you'll say, "No no, I'm fine, go ahead."

We're so scared of being thought pushy, we'd rather delay our entire existence by a minute and a half just to maintain the illusion of courtesy.

And if someone doesn't play the game; if they just storm through the door without a nod or a glance or any acknowledgment of queue law — we remember them. Forever.

"Bit rude."

Said under breath. Probably with a look. Possibly with a quiet "hmph" to whoever we're with.

That's how important it is. It's not about moving. It's about respect. About giving your opponent the chance to decline your offer of politeness before doing the same to you. A stand-off. A power move dressed up as humility.

And when it's finally resolved and someone does go through first? We always say the same thing:

"Thank you."

"Cheers."

"Sorry."

Always sorry. Obviously.

Epilogue

Well, if you've made it this far, congratulations. That means you either quite enjoyed it, or you dropped the book behind the sofa three weeks ago and only just found it again during a half-hearted clean.

Either way, we're here now.

If this book's proved anything, it's that Britain isn't broken. It's just running on biscuits, sarcasm, and passive-aggressive weather chat. We're a nation that queues in silence, nods at strangers for no reason, and says sorry when someone else walks into us. And for some reason, we've all agreed not to mention how weird that is.

But underneath the awkwardness and the rain and the national obsession with bin day, there's something solid. A shared understanding. A quiet agreement that, whatever happens, we'll still stand politely behind someone in Tesco who's paying with pennies and an expired voucher from 1998.

So if any of this rang true, even a bit; if you've ever held a hot cup of tea while the world fell apart around you and thought "ah well, could be worse" — then you're exactly who I wrote this for.

Thanks for reading. I'm off to boil the kettle, argue with the thermostat, and pretend I've got no idea who keeps putting empty wrappers back in the biscuit tin.

Cheers.

Mick

Also by Mick Flaherty

Mick Flaherty is a bestselling author, military veteran, and full-time wordsmith. His writing spans comedy, satire, and career-focused content — from laugh-out-loud books about everyday British nonsense to razor-sharp CVs, LinkedIn profiles, and job applications.

Whether it's helping someone land their next role or pointing out the absurdity of queue etiquette, Mick brings the same no-nonsense tone, down-to-earth style, and dry wit to everything he writes. If it needs words, he's your man. If it needs buzzwords or fluff, he'll probably bin it.

DON'T VOLUNTEER FOR ANYTHING
Don't Volunteer for Anything is a brutally funny, no-nonsense look at military life through the eyes of someone who's done the tours, dodged guard duty, and survived more pointless briefs than hot dinners. Part memoir, part satire, it's packed with real stories, dry humour, and the kind of truths only someone who's served would dare put in print.

Printed in Great Britain
by Amazon